Borreguita and the Coyote

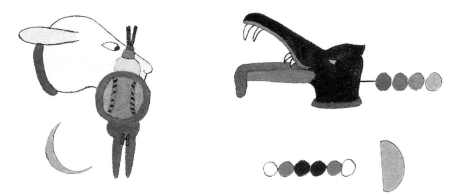

Borreguita and the Coyote

A Tale from Ayutla, Mexico

Retold by Verna Aardema · Illustrated by Petra Mathers

Alfred A. Knopf · New York

THIS IS A BORZOI BOOK PUBLISHED BY ALFRED A. KNOPF, INC.

Text copyright © 1991 by Verna Aardema
Illustrations copyright © 1991 by Petra Mathers
All rights reserved under International and Pan-American Copyright
Conventions. Published in the United States by Alfred A. Knopf, Inc.,
New York, and simultaneously in Canada by Random House of Canada
Limited, Toronto. Distributed by Random House, Inc., New York.

Library of Congress Cataloging-in-Publication Data
Aardema, Verna. Borreguita and the coyote/by Verna Aardema;
illustrated by Petra Mathers.   p.   cm.
Summary: A little lamb uses her clever wiles to
keep a coyote from eating her up.
ISBN 0-679-80921-X (trade)—ISBN 0-679-90921-4 (lib. bdg.)
[1. Folklore—Mexico.]   I. Mathers, Petra, ill. II. Title.
PZ8.1.A213Bo   1991   398.24′597358′0972—dc20 [E]   90-33302 CIP AC
Borreguita and the Coyote: A Tale from Ayutla, Mexico, was translated
and retold by Verna Aardema from "El Borreguita y el Coyote,"
beginning on page 509, with one episode from "La Zorra y el
Coyote," page 514, in *Tales from Jalisco, Mexico,* Vol. XXXV,
by Howard T. Wheeler, published by
The American Folklore Society, 1943.
Grateful acknowledgment is made to the American Folklore
Society for permission to use this translated adaptation.

6 8 0 9 7 5
Manufactured in the U.S.A.
Book Design by Edward Miller

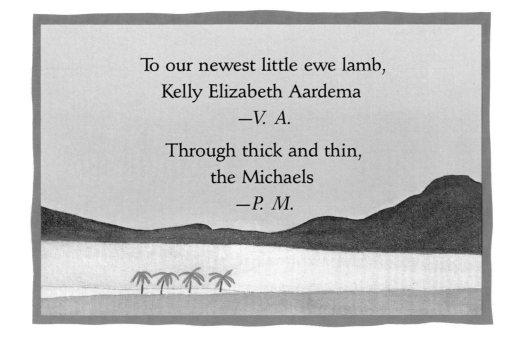

To our newest little ewe lamb,
Kelly Elizabeth Aardema
—*V. A.*

Through thick and thin,
the Michaels
—*P. M.*

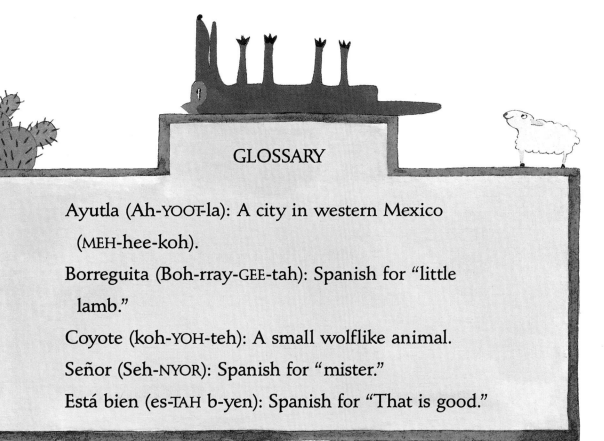

GLOSSARY

Ayutla (Ah-YOOT-la): A city in western Mexico (MEH-hee-koh).

Borreguita (Boh-rray-GEE-tah): Spanish for "little lamb."

Coyote (koh-YOH-teh): A small wolflike animal.

Señor (Seh-NYOR): Spanish for "mister."

Está bien (es-TAH b-yen): Spanish for "That is good."

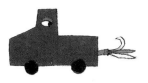

On a farm at the foot of a mountain, there once lived a little ewe lamb. Her master called her simply *Borreguita,* which means "little lamb."

One day Borreguita's master tied her to a stake in a field of red clover. The lamb was eating the lush plants when a coyote came along.

The coyote growled, "*Grrr!* Borreguita, I'm going to eat you!"

Borreguita bleated, "*Baa-a-a-a, baa-a-a-a!* Oh, Señor Coyote, I would not fill you up. I am as thin as a bean pod. When I have eaten all this clover, I shall be fat. You may eat me *then*."

Coyote looked at the skinny little lamb and the wide clover field. "*Está bien.* That is good," he said. "When you are fat, I shall come back."

After many days the coyote returned. He found the lamb grazing in a meadow. He growled, *"Grrr!* Borreguita, you are as plump as a tumbleweed. I'm going to eat you *now!"*

Borreguita bleated, *"Baa-a-a-a, baa-a-a-a!* Sẽnor Coyote, I know something that tastes ever so much better than lamb!"

"What?" asked Coyote.

"Cheese!" cried Borreguita. "My master keeps a round of cheese on his table. He eats it on his tacos."

The coyote had never heard of cheese, and he was curious about it. "How can I get some of this cheese?" he asked.

Borreguita said, "There is a pond at the end of the pasture. Tonight, when the moon is high, meet me there. And I will show you how to get a cheese."

"Está bien," said Coyote. "I will be there."

That night, when the full moon was straight up in the sky, Borreguita and Coyote met at the edge of the pond.

There, glowing in the black water, was something that looked like a big, round cheese.

"Do you see it?" cried Borreguita. "Swim out and get it."

Coyote slipped into the water and paddled toward the cheese. He swam and swam, *shuh, shuh, shuh, shuh*. But the cheese stayed just so far ahead. Finally, he opened his mouth and lunged—WHOOOSH!

The image shattered in the splash!

Pond water rushed into Coyote's mouth. Coughing and spluttering, he turned and headed for the shore.

When he reached it, the little lamb was gone.
She had tricked him! Coyote shook the water off his
fur, *freh, freh, freh.*

Then he looked up at the big cheese in the sky and howled,
"OWOOOOOAH!"

At dawn the next day Borreguita went to graze near a small overhanging ledge of rock on the side of the mountain. She knew that the coyote would be coming after her, and she had a plan.

As the sun rose over the mountain, Borreguita saw the coyote coming. He was sniffing along, with his nose on some trail. She crawled under the ledge and lay on her back, bracing her feet against the top.

When the coyote found her, he growled, *"Grrr!* Borreguita, I see you under there. I'm going to pull you out and eat you!"

Borreguita bleated, *"Baa-a-a-a, baa-a-a-a!* Señor Coyote, you can't eat me *now!* I have to hold up this mountain. If I let go, it will come tumbling down."

The coyote looked at the mountain. He saw that the lamb was holding it up.

"You are strong," said Borreguita. "Will you hold it while I go for help?"

The coyote did not want the mountain to fall, so he crept under the ledge and put up his feet.

"Push hard," said Borreguita. "Do you have it now?"

"I have it," said Coyote. "But hurry back. This mountain is heavy."

Borreguita rolled out of the shallow cave and went leaping and running all the way back to the barnyard.

Coyote held up that rock until his legs ached and he was hungry and thirsty. At last he said, "Even if the mountain falls, I'm going to let go! I can't hold it any longer."

The coyote dragged himself out and covered his head with his paws. The mountain did not fall. Then he knew—the little lamb had fooled him again.

Coyote sat on his haunches and howled, "OWOOOOOAH!"

Early the next morning the coyote hid himself in a thicket in the lamb's pasture. When she drew near, he sprang out with a WOOF! And he said, "Borreguita, you will not escape this time! I'm going to eat you *now!*"

Borreguita bleated, "*Baa-a-a-a, baa-a-a-a!* Señor Coyote, I know I deserve to die. But grant me one kindness. Swallow me whole so that I won't have to suffer the biting and the chewing."

"Why should I make you comfortable while I eat you?" demanded the coyote. "Anyway, I couldn't swallow you all in one piece even if I wanted to."

"Oh, yes, you could!" cried Borreguita. "Your mouth is so big, you could swallow a cougar. Open it wide, and I will run and dive right in."

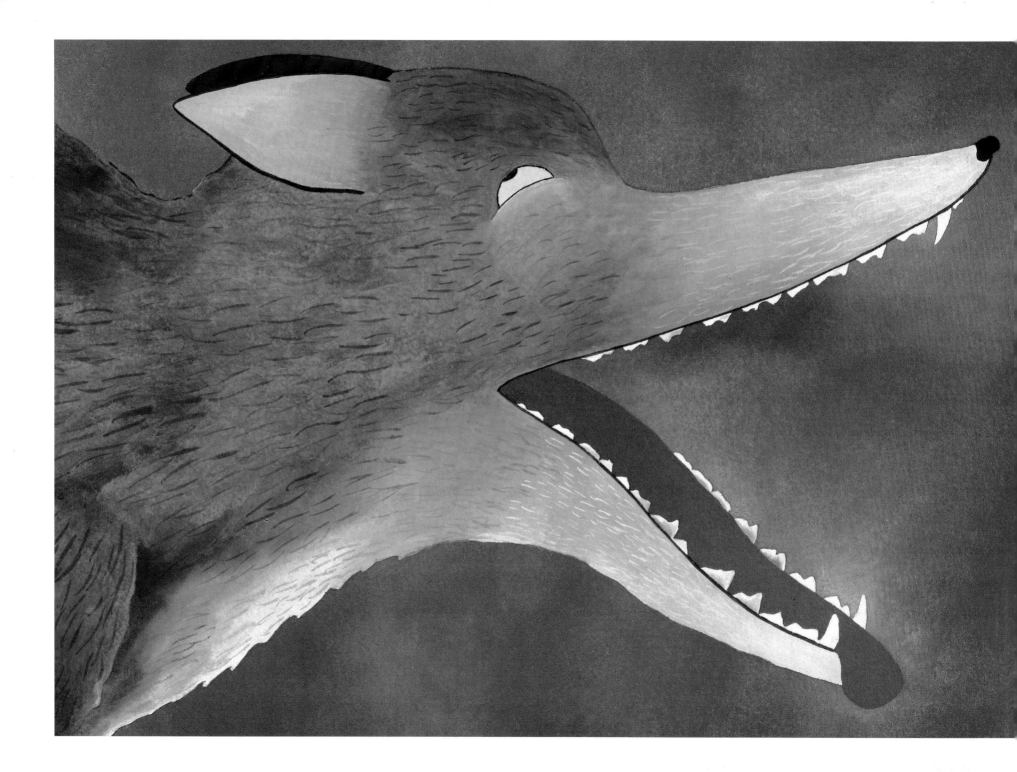

Coyote opened his mouth wide and braced his feet.
Borreguita backed away. Then she put her head down and charged.

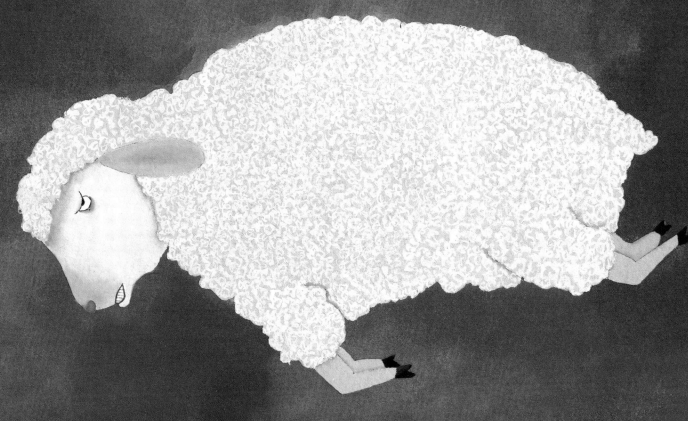

BAM! She struck the inside of Coyote's mouth so hard she sent him rolling.

"OW, OW, OW!" howled the coyote as he picked himself up and ran away—his mouth feeling like one big toothache!

And from that day on, Borreguita frisked about on the farm at the foot of the mountain. And Coyote never bothered her again.

THE END
FIN

Verna Aardema is the award-winning author of many picture books, including *Why Mosquitoes Buzz in People's Ears,* which won the 1976 Caldecott Medal; *Bringing the Rain to Kapiti Plain,* a Reading Rainbow Featured Selection; and, most recently, *Traveling to Tondo* (Knopf). She lives in North Fort Myers, Florida, with her husband.

Petra Mathers is the illustrator of *I'm Flying,* by Alan Wade, which was named a *New York Times* Best Illustrated Book of 1990, and was praised by *Publishers Weekly* for a "visual sophistication [that is] perfectly attuned with the text." Her other titles include two previous *New York Times* Best Illustrated Books, *Theodor and Mr. Balbini* and *Molly's New Washing Machine.* She lives in Portland, Oregon.

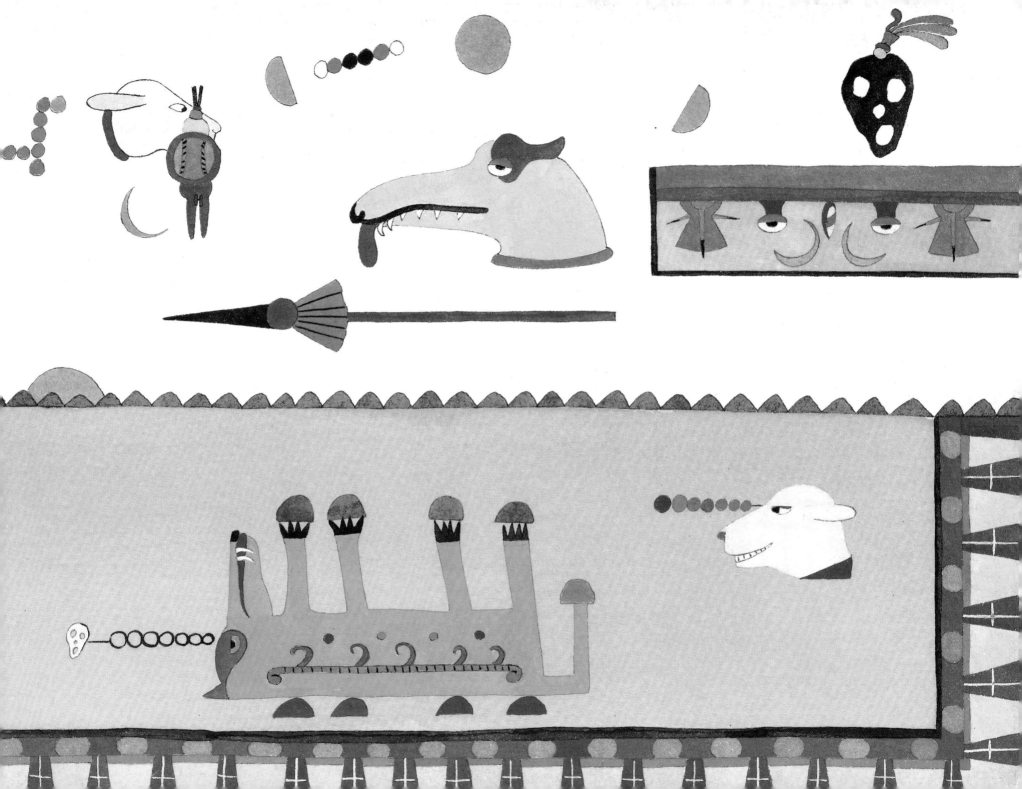